21951

How Georgina Drove the Car
Very Carefully
from Boston to New York

How Georgina Drove the Car Very Carefully from Boston to New York

Lucy Bate

illustrated by

Tamar Taylor

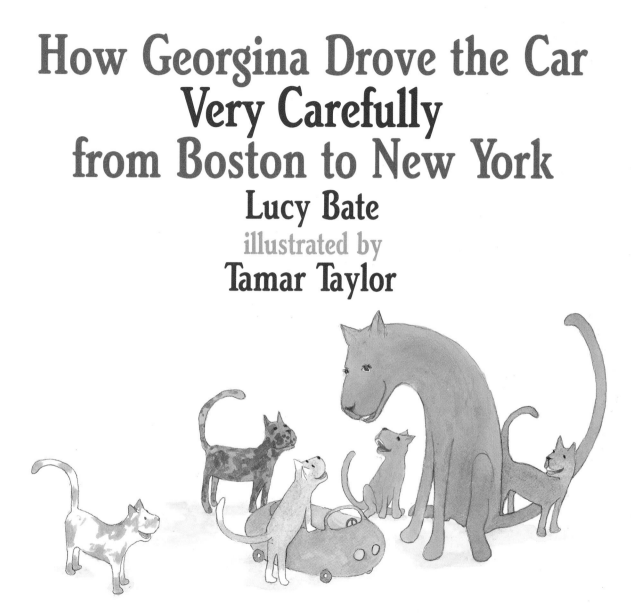

Crown Publishers, Inc.
New York

Published by Crown Publishers, Inc., 225 Park Avenue South, New York, New York 10003 and
represented in Canada by the Canadian MANDA Group.
CROWN is a trademark of Crown Publishers, Inc.
Manufactured in Japan

Library of Congress Cataloging-in-Publication Data
Bate, Lucy. How Georgina drove the car very carefully from Boston to New York
Lucy Bate: illustrated by Tamar Taylor.

Summary: Young Georgina pretends she drives her family all the way from Boston to Grandma's
house in New York City.
    [1. Automobile driving—Fiction.   2. Imagination—Fiction.]
I. Taylor, Tamar, ill.   II. Title.
PZ7.B29427Ho 1988
[E]—dc19

ISBN 0-517-57142-0

10 9 8 7 6 5 4 3 2 1

First Edition

Georgina lives in Boston with her mommy and her daddy
and her sister, Madeline.

Georgina is having a ride.

"Where are you going, Georgina?"

"I'm going to New York City
to see Grandma and Grandpa."

"Are you going on a train?"

"No, I'm going in a car."

"Is Daddy driving the car?" her mother asks.

Georgina says, "No,
I drive the car."

Daddy gets in the car.

Mommy gets in the car.

Madeline

gets in the car.

Kate

and the

kittens get in the car.

Georgina drives very carefully down the street . . .

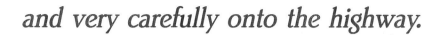

and very carefully onto the highway.

There are some cows.

Madeline says "Hi!" to the cows.

Georgina does not say "Hi!"
because she is very busy
driving carefully.

There are some horses.

Madeline waves to the horses.

Georgina does not wave. She is very busy driving carefully.

Georgina is hungry.

She stops at a restaurant.

Everybody
has lunch.
They have . . .

popcorn

bananas

artichokes

chocolate chip

cheese sandwiches

ice cream

chocolate
chip cookies

white milk

chocolate milk

cherries
and
hotdogs.

Edinbrook Elem. Media
ISD No. 279
8925 Zane Ave. N.
Brooklyn Park, MN 55443

Georgina pays for the lunch.

She buys balloons with the change.

Daddy doesn't want a balloon, so Georgina buys him a truck.

Mommy doesn't want a truck,

so Georgina buys her some buttons.

The family goes back to the car.

They give Kate and the kittens
some milk and a sardine sandwich
without bones.

Then Georgina starts the car again and drives all the way to New York.

She only stops for a red light,

a stop sign,

Here is Grandma
and Grandpa's street.
Georgina parks the car.
Here are Grandma and Grandpa.

"Hi, Grandma! Hi, Grandpa!"

"Hello, Georgina. Hello, Madeline."

Grandpa says, "Who drove the car?"

"I drove the car," says Georgina.

"**You** drove the car?!
Did you drive very carefully?"

Georgina says,
"I drove **very** carefully."

"You must be tired," Grandma says.

"Come in, come in."

Georgina and Madeline put on their nightgowns

and brush their teeth.

"I am going to drive next," Madeline says.

"I didn't have a turn."

Georgina says, "Okay."